Help the mice find their way home. Draw a line for them to follow.

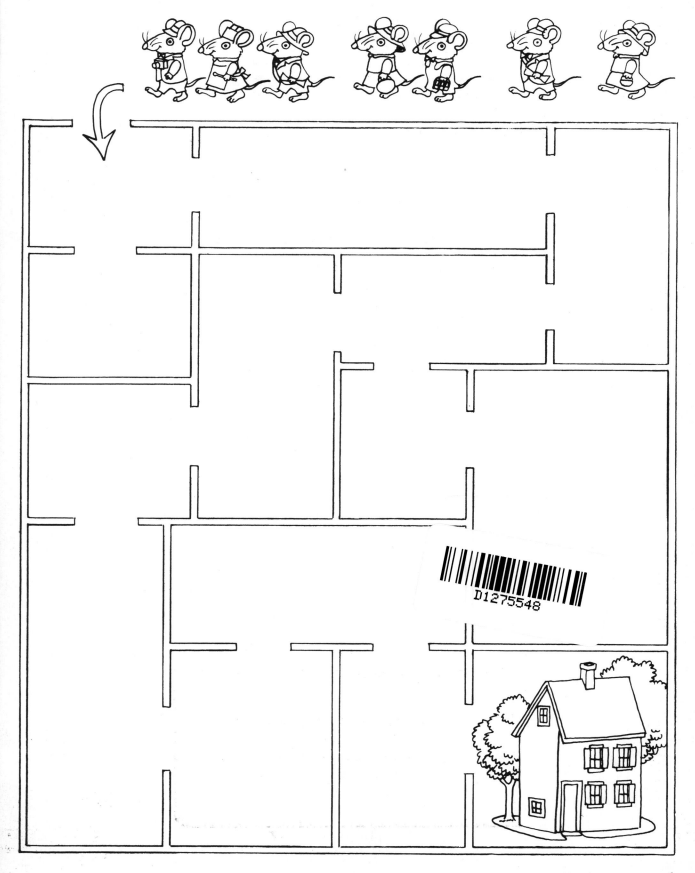

Count how many are in each set.
Say the name of the number. Write the numbers.

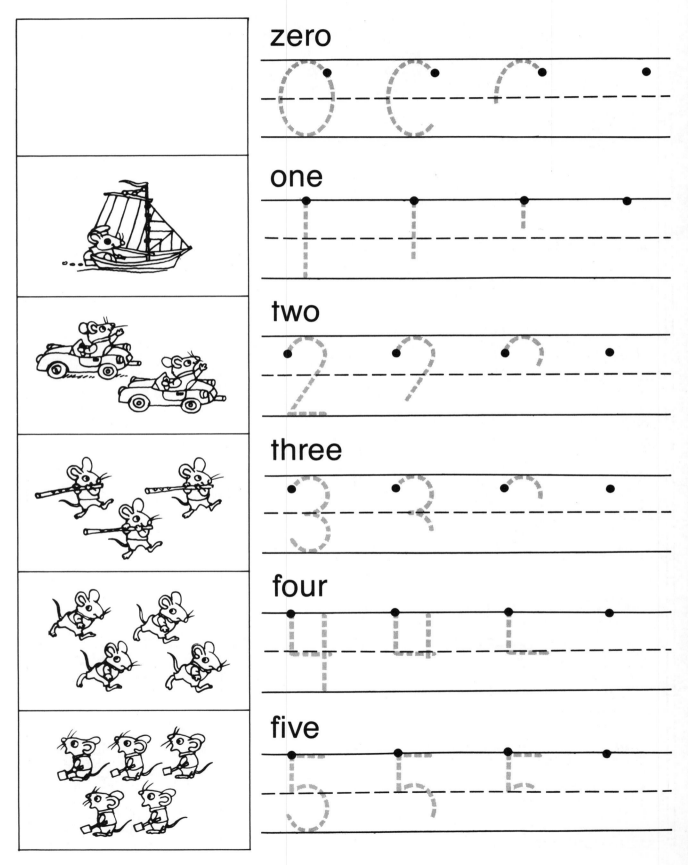

zero

one

two

three

four

five

How many are in each set? Write the number in the box.

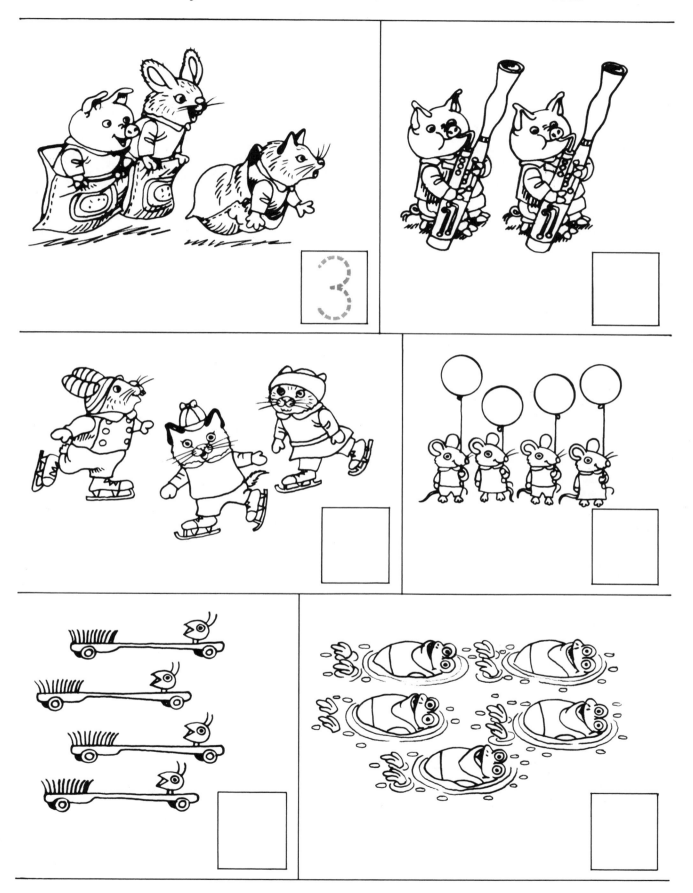

Look at the numbers below the set.
Draw a circle around that many to make smaller sets.

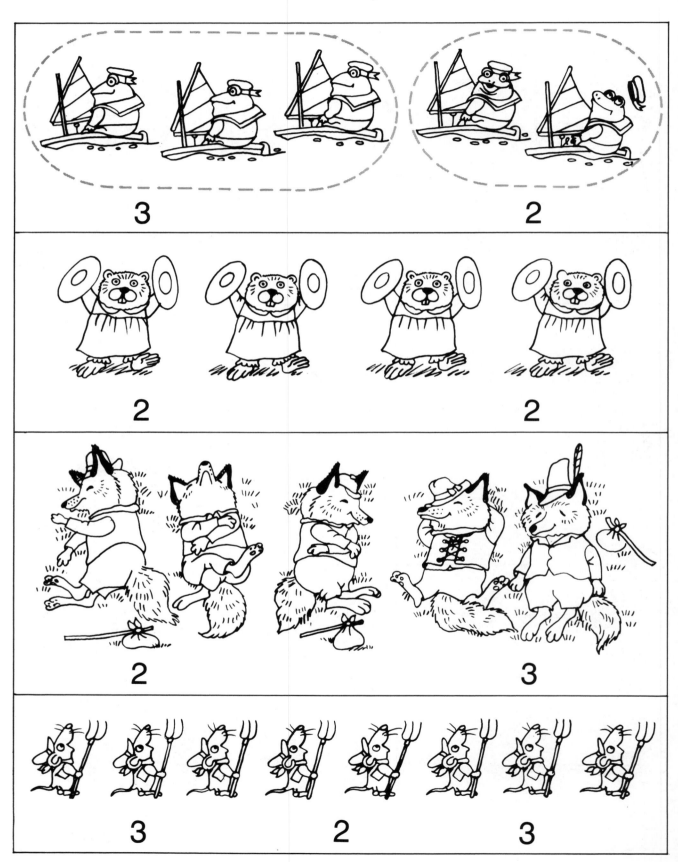

3   2

2   2

2   3

3   2   3

Count each set. Draw a line connecting the sets with the same number.

Look at the number in the box. Draw a circle around that many boats.

2

5

4

3

3

Count. Write the number in the box.

"Cluck! Cluck!"
See the eggs in the hen's nest.
How many are there?

How many eggs
are in this nest?

Becky Bunny is pulling
her wagon along.
How many apples does Becky Bunny
have in her wagon?

My, what a beautiful cake!
Take a deep breath, Lowly. . . and BLOW!
Count the candles on Lowly's cake.

How many ice cream cones does Roger Raccoon have? Draw that many in the box.

How many cans of paint does Lowly have?
Draw that many in the box.

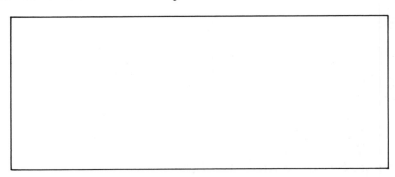

How many apples are on the scale?
Draw that many in the box.

How many hearts do you see?
Draw that many in the box.

Count how many are in each set.
Say the name of the number. Write the numbers.

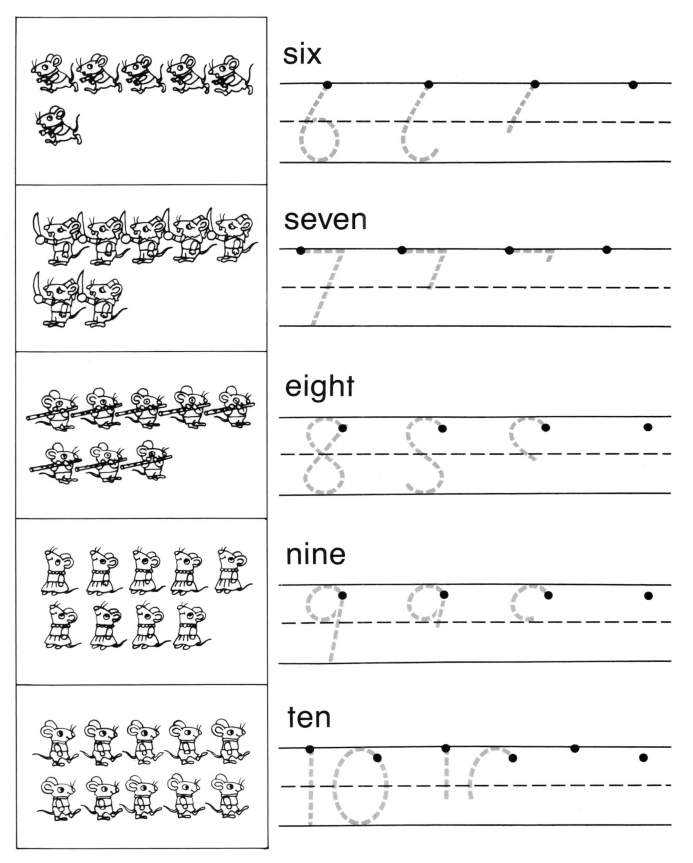

six

seven

eight

nine

ten

How many are in each set? Write the number in the box.

Ask a grownup to color the crayons.
Color all spaces with three dots green. Color all spaces with four dots blue.
Color all spaces with five dots red, and color all spaces with six dots yellow.

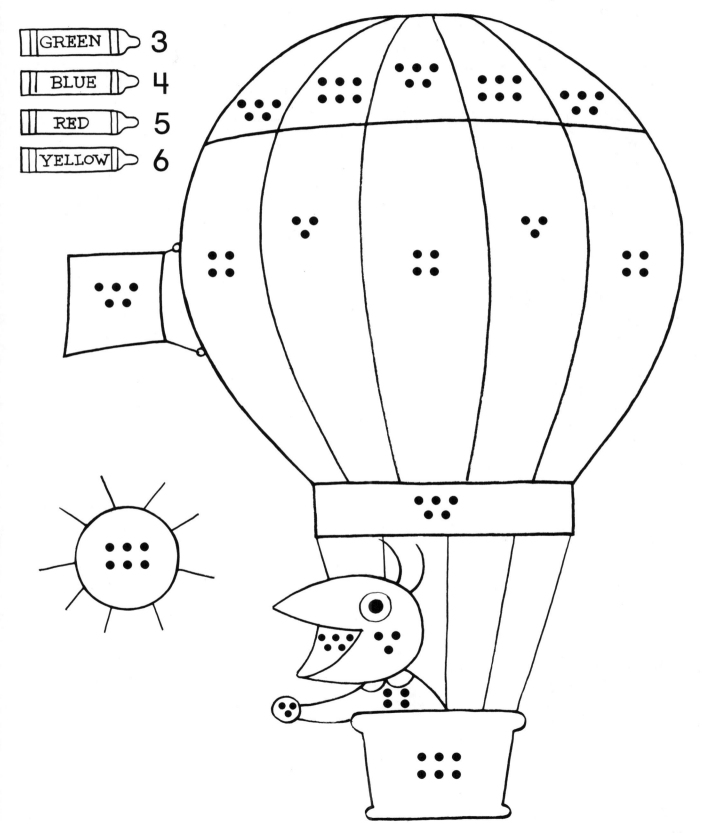

How many are in each set? Write the number in the box.

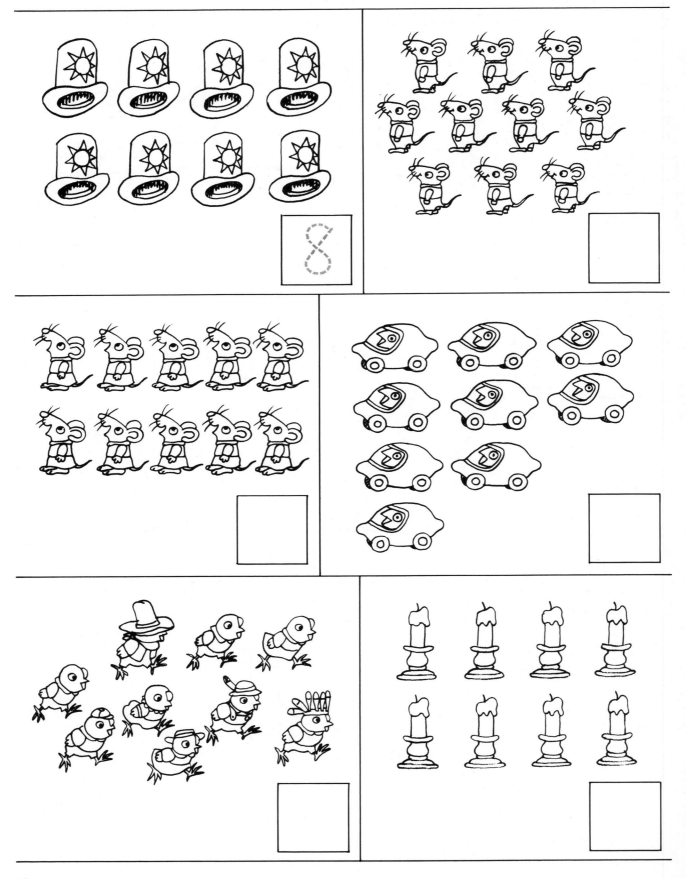

It's apple-picking time. How many apples did each child pick?
Follow the line from each child to the apples. Count that many apples.
Write the number in the box above the child.

Connect the dots in order. Color the picture.

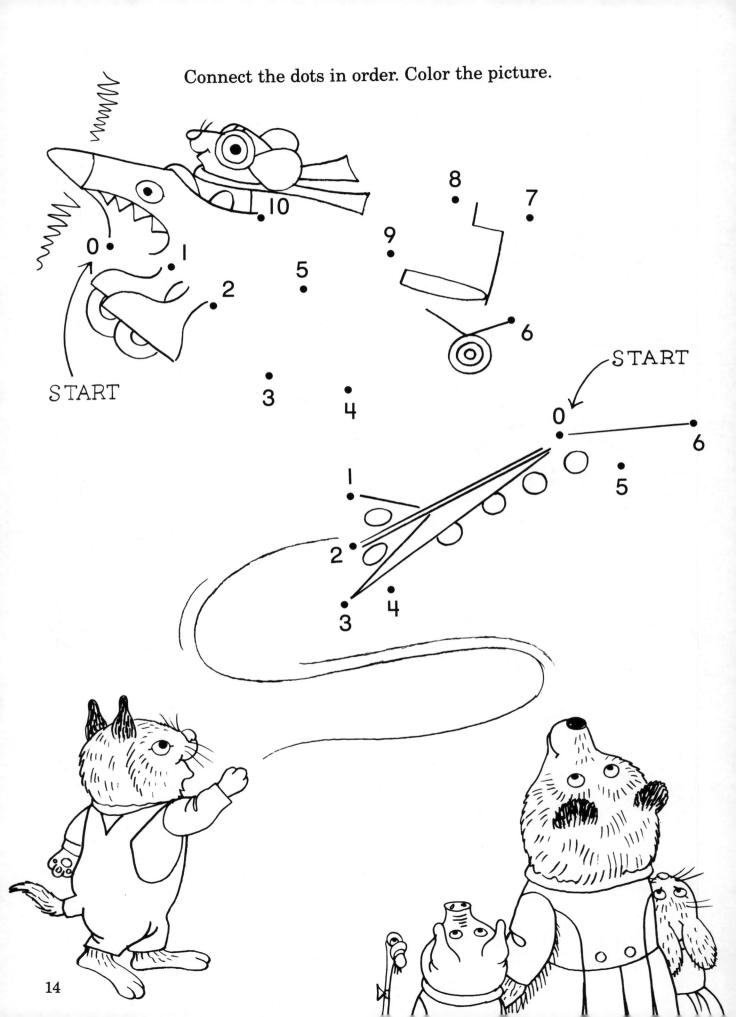

8

7

9

5

10

0

1

2

START

3

4

6

START

0

6

1

5

2

3

4

Count. Draw a line connecting each set with the matching number.

5

8

6

4

7

9

15

Find a path home for each of the children.
Follow all the boxes with a 4 and color them red for Rachel Rabbit.
Follow all the boxes with a 6 and color them blue for Peter Pig.

Hurry on home!
Your mother's calling you!

4							6
4	4	4	2	5	3	6	6
3	5	4	4	9	8	6	2
7	3	2	4	5	7	6	9
	8	4	6	6	6	8
	9	4	6	5	9	3
4	5	7	4	6	7	
4	4	4	4	6	6	

Count. Write the number in the box.

Oops! Lowly was driving too fast.
He crashed into an apple tree.
How many apples fell to the ground?

How many jars of jelly
is the juggler juggling?

Ruth Rabbit is making a daisy
chain. How many daisies are
in the chain?

My, what a lot of fire fighters!
How many fire fighters
are putting out the fire?

Separate the set into smaller sets. Draw a line.

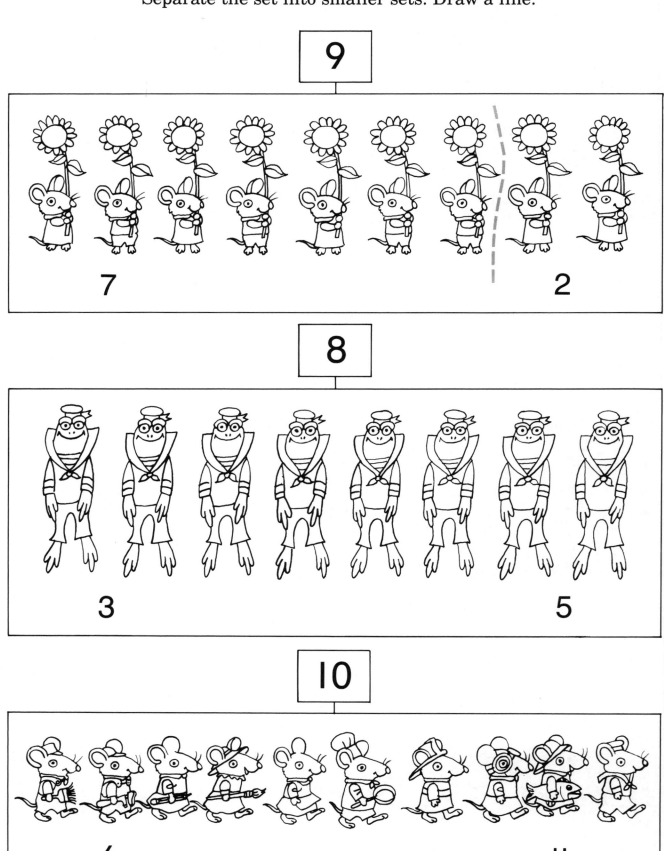

9

7   2

8

3   5

10

6   4

Ask a grownup to color the crayons.
Color all spaces with a 5 red. Color all spaces with a 6 yellow.
Color all spaces with a 7 green, and color all spaces with an 8 brown.

5 | RED
6 | YELLOW
7 | GREEN
8 | BROWN

The children are waiting in line for the school bus.
Huckle is first in line. Lowly Worm is fourth.

| 1 | 2 | 3 | 4 | 5 |
| first | second | third | fourth | fifth |

Draw a circle around the second child.

Draw an X on the third child.

Color the fifth child.

left 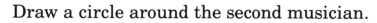 **right**

Draw a circle around the second musician.

Draw a line under the fifth clock.

Draw an X on the third pig.

Draw a circle around the first flower.

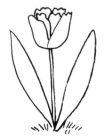    

11
eleven

Now that you can count to 10, let's go on.

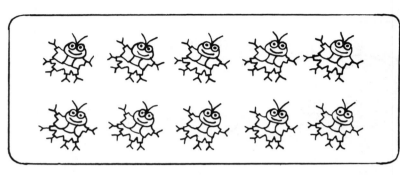

Here is a set of 10.

Add 1 more.
10 and 1 make a set of 11.

Write the number.

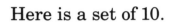

12
twelve

Add 1 more.
10 and 2 make a set of 12.

Write the number.

13
thirteen

Add 1 more.
10 and 3 make a set of 13.

Write the number.

14
fourteen

Add 1 more.
10 and 4 make a set of 14.

Write the number.

Trace the numbers
on the clock face.

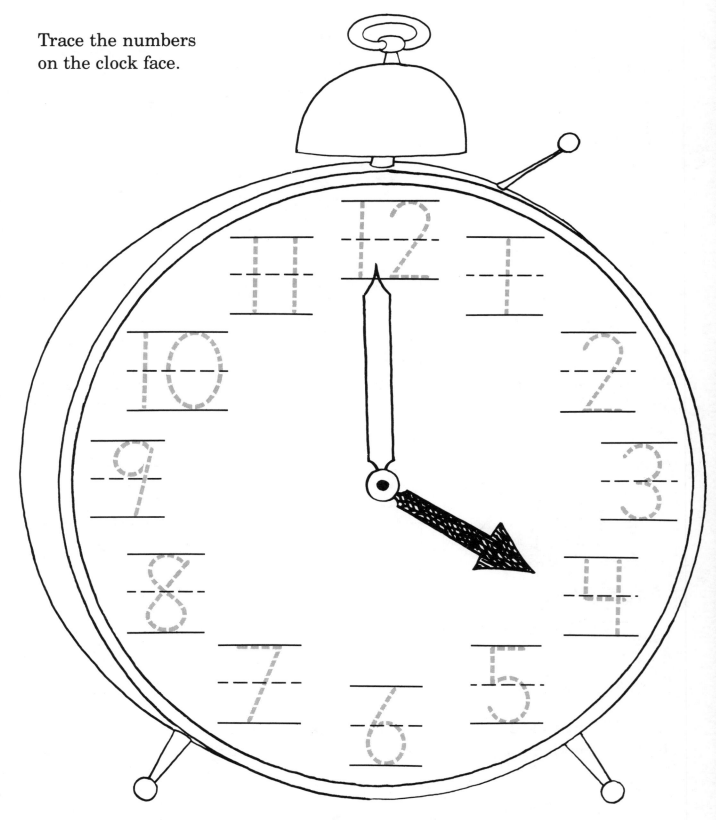

The minute hand is the long hand. It tells the number of minutes.
It is at the 12. When it is at the 12, it is o'clock.
The short hand is the hour hand. It tells the hours. It is at the 4.

The time is **4** o'clock.

It is Saturday and there is no school.
Huckle has lots to do. You can see what time he does things.
Look at the clock. Then write that time.

At __7__ o'clock Huckle bounces out of bed. Lowly arrives to visit for the day.

At _____ o'clock Huckle eats his breakfast.

At _____ o'clock they shop for food with Mother Cat.

At _____ o'clock noon Huckle and Lowly eat lunch.

At _____ o'clock Huckle and Lowly take a nap.

At _____ o'clock they play in the muddy yard.

Count. Write the numbers.

15
fifteen

10 and 5 make a set of 15.

16
sixteen

10 and 6 make a set of 16.

17
seventeen

10 and 7 make a set of 17.

Count. Write the numbers.

18
eighteen

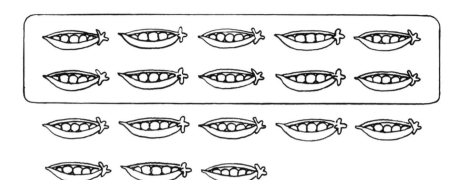

10 and 8 make a set of 18.

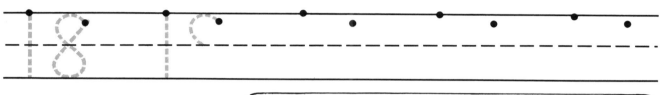

19
nineteen

10 and 9 make a set of 19.

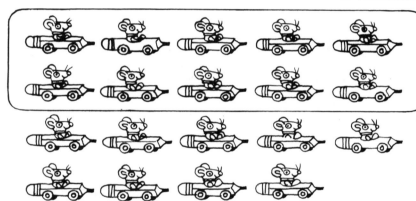

20
twenty

10 and 10 make a set of 20.

27

Count how many. Write the number in the box.

13

Write the missing numbers on the boxcars.

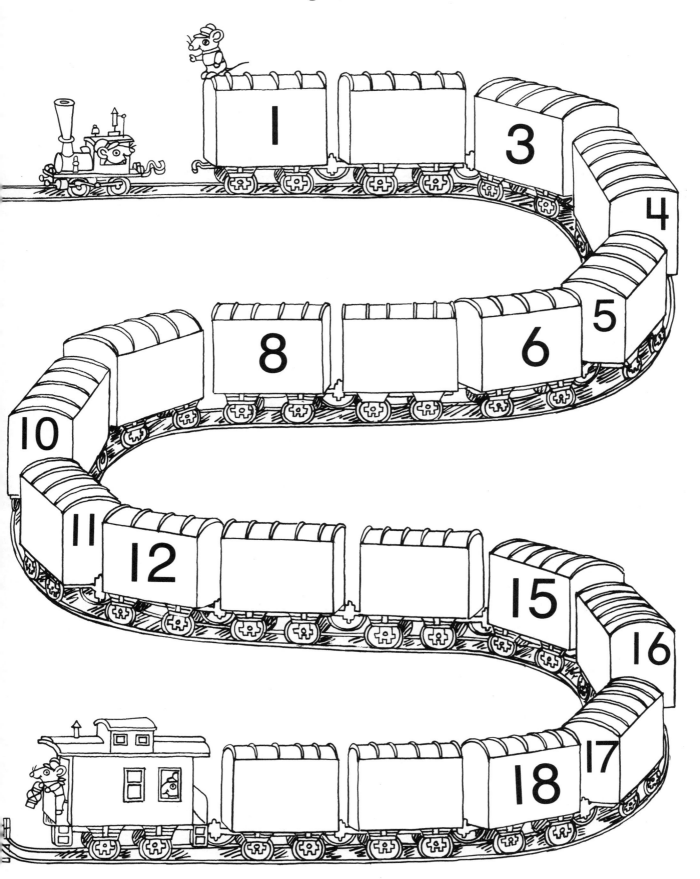

Connect the dots in order to see who is under the umbrella.

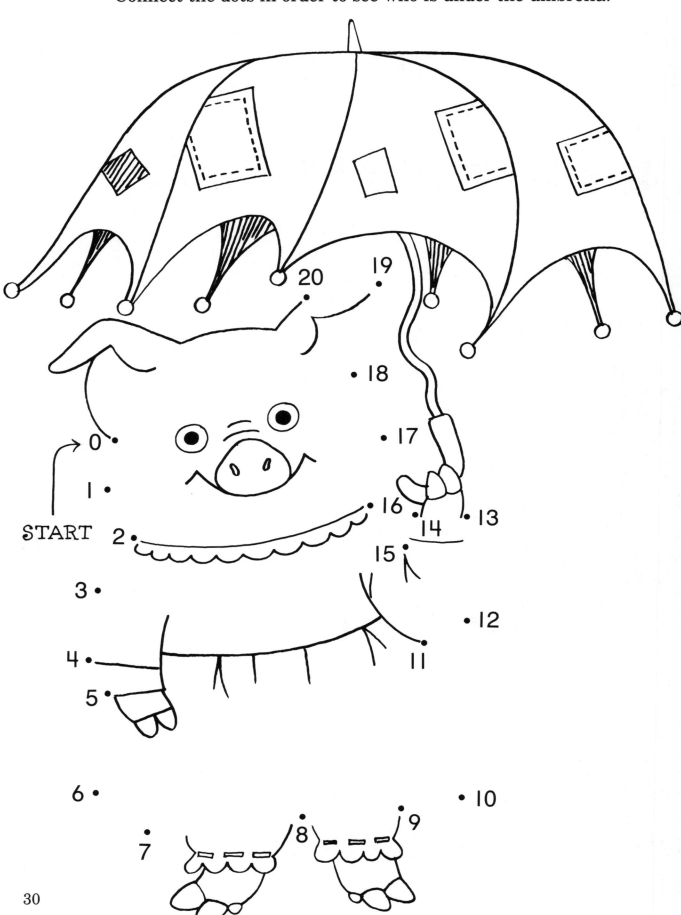

START

Let's learn to count by 10.

10

1 2 3 4 5 6 7 8 9 10

20 has
2 sets of 10.

1 2 3 4 5 6 7 8 9 10

11 12 13 14 15 16 17 18 19 20

30 has
3 sets of 10.

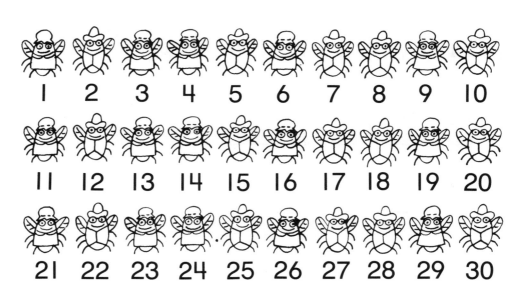

1 2 3 4 5 6 7 8 9 10

11 12 13 14 15 16 17 18 19 20

21 22 23 24 25 26 27 28 29 30

Trace the numbers.

21 22 23 24 25

26 27 28 29 30

Count by 10 to 100.

| 10 | 20 | 30 | 40 | 50 | 60 | 70 | 80 | 90 | 100 |
| ten | twenty | thirty | forty | fifty | sixty | seventy | eighty | ninety | one hundred |

Write the missing numbers.

1	2	3	4	5	6	7	8	9	10
11									20
21									30
31									40
41									50
51									60
61									70
71									80
81									90
91									100